Someone Has To Pay

Rolita James

Copyright © 2021 Rolita James

The content contained within this book may not be reproduced, duplicated, or transmitted without direct written permission from the author or the publisher.

DEDICATION

I dedicate this book to my children, De'borah, Dominique, David Jr., and my grandson, Scoop. Also, anyone who has experienced any part of this plan, process, or promise. Lastly, to anyone who found themselves in my pages of life.

CONTENTS

DEDICATION..2

FORWARD 5

INTRODUCTION..10

CHAPTER 1 1

AND SO IT BEGINS...1

CHAPTER 2 9

WHILE BLEEDING...9

CHAPTER 3 21

A WAY TO MAKE IT..21

CHAPTER 4 27

REGGIE 27

CHAPTER 5 38

WHO WANTS TO MARRY A MILLIONAIRE?............38

CHAPTER 6 50

WHEN EVERYBODY LOVES YOU BUT ME...............50

CHAPTER 7 58

PROMISES, PROMISES...58

CHAPTER 8 67

UNIVERSITY OF HARD KNOCKS 67

CHAPTER 9 74

THE TOUCH... 74

CHAPTER 10 83

FANTASY AND THE FATE 83

CHAPTER 11 91

ON MY OWN... 91

Forward

I met Rolita over 30 years ago in Stamford, CT, when we were just 18 years old. Rolita's grandmother and my aunt were the best of friends. When we met my aunt introduced her by her nickname "Tina-baby". I was this quiet shy girl from Florida and she was this boisterous, no-nonsense, outspoken girl that would fight anybody in a heartbeat LOL. Her favorite saying was "I'll punch you in the throat". I was so enamored with her personality because she wasn't afraid of anything or anyone.

Over the years I have watched Rolita face so many disappointments in her life: the passing of loved ones, divorce, cancer, losing her home, being betrayed by family and friends, and many other sorrows in her life. What I discovered about her she is truly a fighter, I watched as God began to burn away those rough edges transforming her from the inside out showing her unconditional love and teaching her how to forgive. Rolita has taken those adversities and shifted her entire life. She is walking in the calling that God has placed on her life. Rolita is a phenomenal Pastor, mom, grandma, friend, and leader. She is truly a testament of God's redemption plan.

Pastor Rolita James will walk you through any difficulty, hardships, or tragedy with love, compassion, and no judgment. Her church "A Passion for the Truth Church" has helped hundreds of people turn their lives around.

This book you will not be able to put down!! If you're ready for healing and freedom this is for you. You will definitely want to tell your family and friends to get this book, it is a must read.

-Valerie Knight

Do you know Rolita James? I do. I knew her as a young woman. Even though our times were different, as young people we both walked the same sidewalks and hung out on the same corners in the same neighborhood, and we both absorbed into our conscience the DNA of a culturally and socially diverse West Side.

Rolita's book will give the reader a firsthand introspection of a young woman who faced hardship on her own starting at a young age. The way she describes her trials and tribulations reads almost like a novel. From the first line and throughout the entire read her life story is captivating and unique.

Rolita had a much more difficult childhood. Her everyday path as a young adult presented a challenge which is why her growth and development into the amazing adult woman she is makes it nothing less than astonishing. As difficult as things were for her personally, she never left anyone who needed help behind. My empathy and understanding of how she struggled gives and to what she has become in the community has earned my greatest admiration and respect.

That's just half the story.

How did the author become who she is today? Where did her incredible people skills, her powerful preaching, her gifted song, her love of others and her kind, inviting nature all come from? How did she go from the street to

God and to become a sought after advisor and confidant, a determined problem solver and friend and one of the most uniquely interesting people you will ever engage.

You will read about Queenie, her Godfather and the woman with the Island accent. These were the people who had a powerful influence on who Rolita is and what she has become. As you read further you will learn how these people had an everlasting effect on her.

In Queenie she saw the face of God. Queenie was an incredible woman. Queenie was a poor woman who struggled with life and yet found time to adopt children including Rolita. Queenie made a way, not only for herself but for Rolita as well. There is no telling what would have happened if Queenie had not brought divine intervention to Rolita's life. I did not know Queenie but must love her for all she has been able to do from just her giving heart.

The author tells us how she recognized building blocks in her young life and drew upon them into her adult life. Today Rolita is a successful woman accomplished in her role. She is strong, passionate, professional, kind, hard working, creative, and in love not only with her congregation but with her entire community and her community with her.

-Michael A. Pavia,

Former Mayor of

Stamford CT. 2009 to 2013

Introduction

Written within these pages are my innermost thoughts and emotions expressed through poetic and life phrases.

Consider all that is written. They are my innermost self, my desires, fantasies, issues, visions, longings, and wants.

You have inspired me!
Stirring up and arousing an intellect and wisdom that I have hidden for many years.

You've stimulated emotions I thought were no longer alive or even present with me.

Agape, not Eros.

Ponder all within carefully.

-Rolita James

Chapter 1

And So It Begins

"What chu call yaself doing?"

Life for me ain't been no crystal stair, at least that's what the poem said. Even though I'm in her belly, the brown liquid found its way into here too. **"Ready or not, here I come, you can't hide, gonna find you and take my time."** The brown liquor, like Freddy Krueger, had a habit of sneaking up on her, easing its way down my mother's throat, ready to devour what God placed in her womb.

The brown liquor met her at work, squatting behind a car seat and sitting on the stoop blending in with the rest of 'em. Jack Daniels, Captain Morgan, Johnny Walker, or any other dark liquor always did a number on her. I imagine it wanted to devour me too.

I'm in a warm place, feeling safe being carried by Flawless. Flawless was one of the most beautiful women that God had ever handcrafted. But why is she so broken? Everybody loves her. Her friends swear by her kindness and loyalty. She was fearless and was even known to knock out a few men in her day. Her record is about 15-0. Her house was "the house." You know, the one that hosted all of the parties. What more could Flawless want?

Who is that laughing? Who is he, and why is he singing "Can't get enough of your love babe?" His voice is deep and seductive in tone. "You're my first, my last, my everything." "I love me some Barry White," she said. Who in the heck is Barry White? I wondered. Uh oh, move, buddy, two is enough, and three's a crowd. There's a massage down there below on Flawless near my head. Her hesitation was interpreted as her playing hard to get, and it fueled his desire. The warmth of his quiet breath embraced her flawless caramel skin. His moan was the compass that drew her into the clutches of his manly arms. Why is this man saying that he doesn't want to poke me in the head? I'm beginning to feel dizzy. That brown liquid caught up with me. I'm tired, so I doze off, unsure if I was intoxicated from the motions between Flawless and the man or the brown liquor again.

"Baby, I can't stay. You know if I could, I would; a man has gotta do, what a man has gotta do. I will be back to check up on you and the kids next weekend." Flawless was quiet. And quiet wasn't good. The man knew it, and I knew it too. "Girl, don't act like that," he said, as he kissed Flawless on her forehead. "Come on now, look at me," he murmured as he lifted his big strong hand to place it on Flawless' chin. Their eyes locked, and once again, he secured his position in her heart, life, and bed. Slowly sliding his tongue out to gently lick Flawless's lips, he slid her a couple of dollars. "I'll be back - to protect my investment," he said as he grabbed his coat. "KO, just

Someone Has to Pay   Rolita James

Go!", Flawless said in her flirtatious voice, pushing him gently in the stomach. "KO, Get Out! Call me when you get home." The door closes behind KO. Flawless leans on the door, love-stricken, then startled by the weak doorbell that sounds like a toy horn at a child's party. Flawless opens the door. KO sticks his head in, "Ok, one more." "Bye Boy!" echoes into the hallway as they part ways.

Flawless and I are stressed out. It's October 20, 1968. I can't take being upside down, nor can she handle the pressure. And what does she do? She grabs the brown liquor. Mama, why are you still drinking? I'm ready to come out. The Dr. Thingy is only a few blocks away. One, Two, Three, Four, Five, Six, Seven, Eight, Nine…Ten; ready or not, here I come, you can't hide, gonna find you and take my time. I'm stressing out. Here comes that stuff again. Oh great, now I'm sleepy and queasy again. The brown liquor found me. I have a little fight left, just enough to exit Flawless. They named me Bijou Baby. Reeva, Jacy, Kahlil, Megan, and Denim stood over me in the make-shift bed Flawless put together using her dresser drawer. "I love her, but when is she leaving to go home?" one of them said.

Someone Has to Pay — Rolita James

Two years later, I'm sitting on the tar split playground with broken glass, monkey bars, hopscotch, and the benches with carved out words like "2Gether 4Ever" and "Sharon was here" in the Terrace Housing Projects with no clothes on; just like the day my presence was announced. Flawless was too busy to notice I was outside with my jewels revealed for all the housing projects to see. Somebody called somebody, and before I knew it, Auntie pulled up. She stepped out of the car wearing her Pam Grier wig, white Cooley High wide-heeled pumps, and cropped black leather jacket that fell precisely to her waist. Her waist and curves are defined to perfection in her black Ann Klein slacks. She picks me up, feeling helpless due to her inability to change this situation. Not sure if the Flawless that she loves, respects, and fears, the one who had beat people up on her behalf, would say thank you or blow the entire ordeal out of proportion. With me in her arms, Auntie headed towards building seven. She waited for the elevator, which seemed like it was taking forever. Auntie was not smiling. She stepped over a puddle of urine and walked up six flights of stairs towards Flawless's apartment.

At last, we made it to the fifth floor to find the elevator door wide open because Khalil and Denim were playing in the elevator shaft. "Get your a** down from that shaft! You could have killed yourselves". Khalil jumped through the emergency square from the ceiling, and Denim hung for a few seconds, afraid to jump at four years old. Auntie popped Khalil on the back of his head. "Someone could have been hurt!" Auntie yelled with me still in her arms, frantically ringing the doorbell. I knew Auntie was upset, but there was no indication of her aggravation when the music met us as the door opened. Auntie was mad at Flawless, but she did not convey what she was really thinking. When she walked into the apartment, she was met by the disco lights from the floor model stereo and a kiss on the cheek. "Hey girl," they said to one another.

The aroma of white rice, brown gravy, collard greens, ham hocks with a steak in the oven, laughter, and smoke filled the air. Flawless opened the oven door to base the juicy marinated steak, and the phone rang. She reaches for the phone that is hanging on the wall and answers it. In a fraction of a second, Denim runs over and sits on the oven door. Out comes the steak juice searing Denim's back, taking her caramel flesh with it. Two hours later, Denim is in a full-body cast. Denim's incident should have been the end of the party at Flawless apartment. Still, the party continued, with a two-year-old, a child in a body cast, and four other children running around.

I am now three years old, holding the hand of this tall caramel-complected man with the perfect afro. He had confidence about him and held my hand tight as we walked down the street to the corner store in Southfield Village. I was so happy; I got a whole bag of penny candies. On our way back, KO and Flawless connected. My eyes couldn't help but look up and watch one of the most sensual moments between two individuals, interrupted by tears and words of thanks to KO for moving us to Stamford. Unbeknownst to me, the penny candies would be the last thing KO bought me… because I never thought I would see my dad, KO, again. The compass of his soul led him back to his wife and six children.

One chilly day in April, a year and a half later, Flawless tells Jacy to go to the hardware store to get a long red tube. Back then, we couldn't ask questions, so she did as she was told. Jacy brings it back and gives the tube to Flawless. Flawless goes into the bathroom and inserts the red tube inside her. She aborted KO's twins. Flawless came out of the bathroom wrapped in a charcoal grey wool blanket. She was shivering and bleeding. Jacy, then thirteen, looked on in horror. Paralyzed by fear and disbelief, she wanted to help Flawless but was too mummified by what was happening. I don't remember who called the ambulance, but they came and took her away. I stood helpless and sad in puddles of blood, not knowing that it would be the last time I would see Flawless. You see, the only thing Flawless about Flawless, was her skin.

Chapter 2

While Bleeding

"Every eye closed ain't sleep."

I sat reminiscing about the bright green, bright red, white, and blue Christmas lights in the living room windows of some project high-rise apartments, watching people get off of the Southfield city bus with so many presents. Some they had to carry in their hands, and others they had to push on foot. I wondered what we were getting for Christmas but I was suddenly distracted by the highway games I used to play with my family and friends, Jacy, Kahlil, Megan, Denim, and them. "Punch car! That's my car!"

Punch car was when you saw a Buggie on I-95, you would punch the person next to you and say "punch car!" There would be three to five of them that would ride by at a time; go figure! You had to be quick and first. Every time you saw a Jaguar, Mercedes, Lincoln, or a fancy car; you'd have to yell, "That's my car!" Whoever had the most cars would win. Whatever happened to those days? I thought we made those games up until I found out they were universal. Remember when pebbles were whatever you wanted them to be? Pebbles were marbles or known as a ball and we would find a stick because we couldn't afford a bat. That's what we considered playing baseball. And God only knows who else put the rock in the bike's wheels. How about when you couldn't afford chalk, so we used a stone to draw a hopscotch board? Do you remember the red light, the green light? I escaped the pain through ignorance, adolescence, and the protection of my Grandmother, Queenie.

As I stared across the playground at our old apartment building where my Mom gave herself an abortion I felt sad and alone. I looked over at my Grandmother only to identify with that same look of pain showing on her face. I just didn't know her pain was for a different reason at the time: Queenie was overwhelmed with two jobs, eight of her own children, one of them dead, one daughter kidnapped, living with the pain that her one and only son is in jail while raising three little ones as well as three teenagers that her eldest daughter left behind. On top of all of this, we were robbed of all of our Christmas gifts. Who would do some heartless s*** like that? Bitter-sweet memories.

So why was it bitter-sweet? The day we were robbed, Queenie was also overjoyed. When she sat in her lazy chair and began opening the mail, she got a notice from The Housing Authority that she was eligible to upgrade and move to another housing complex. Yes, indeed, a more sophisticated place with upstairs and downstairs in the apartment. No more high-rise apartments. We were moving up with George and Weezy. Lol

Bernie's was the grocery store next to the projects. On Christmas Eve, Queenie was pushing our belongings over the bridge in Bernie's shopping cart, heading down Wilson Street to High Street to 25 Tillman Place in a snowstorm. You know the wheels get stuck in the store; can you imagine what they were like in a snowstorm with a television, tables, chairs, clothes, pots, and pans?
How many trips do you think we had to make to move everything?

Like clockwork, the alarm would come on. The Star-Spangled Banner on volume ten fills the house from Queenie's room at 6:00 am. She would sit on the edge of her bed with the Bible in her hand, reading her daily scriptures and then falling to her knees with such gratitude.

"Father, I thank you for this day. You've been so good to me. You have been better to me than I have been to myself. Please forgive me as I forgive those who have done me dirty. Save my children, Lawd! Cover my Grandchern Jesus! Keep them from danger seen and unseen."

Seven days a week for as long as you lived in her house, The Star-Spangled Banner would start your day's journey: school, choir rehearsal, usher board, color-guard, Mother Gingiddy's Tuesday Bible study in the basement around the front, doing your chores and getting our long reddish-brown hair washed and pressed. The house had to be spotless because we were the Icy people; you know the frozen flavored water you just had to have in the summer time? Queenie kept a hustle. That icy money bought us a new washing machine and refrigerator.

It feels like yesterday that my best friend Devin and I were running as fast as we could. His freckles turned red while his carrot-orange hair was pressed against his scalp by the wind. I am booked, lol (that's when you run so fast that your feet hit your butt while you're running) while my hair made reddish-brown from the sun, is not moving at all. I was beaten up because I wanted to help some mentally challenged kids out with their arts and craft, and Devin scared them and then slapped one of their art projects down to the ground. I'm trying to help them pick up the pieces of the shattered mug when I hear "run!"

Devin is screaming, running, and laughing so hard until he's gasping for air. "For what?" I say with my head down, picking up the broken but hard worked-on cup, not noticing that some angry Special Ed kids are standing behind me. One kid punched me in the back. I slowly turned my head with my eyes as wide as the Grand Canyon thinking to myself, what did this boy get us into? And then a retarded girl slaps me in the face. "Now, wait a minute, I am on your side," I say this as I'm backing up to state my case like an attorney or a politician. Suddenly, ten of them started chasing me. I am not cut out for this today with my pretty spring pink, lavender, leafy green and ivory floral dress. Not to mention, the finishing touch: my black patent leather church shoes. I slid into a split, and they caught up to me and tore me up.

I couldn't fight them back because they were mentally challenged. I've always wanted to help out in their

Special Olympics. Devin yells from a distance - "run! You will not make it out alive," still laughing uncontrollably with both hands on his knees. I crawl away and take off with a scraped-up knee, heading South of Meadow School past Doug's house, across the Street from the School, past the Golf course, and straight past Stoke Blvd.

It dawns on me, Wait! Why am I running? This is a long way from my house. I decide to catch the school bus. Influenced by this fool. He's off running again, his hair pressed against his scalp from the wind. This time he is chased by some black kids from Wynne Dance Circle, all because he is white. Is this karma for what he did to those special education kids? We slide into the housing complex.

Now I'm screaming, run! Devin Run! Run into my house. They are not going to bother me. Exhausted from this ordeal, we make it to my house, and Devin slid into the door like a New York Yankee player with bases loaded. As he plops down on the couch, he sits on what he thinks is a black baby doll which happens to be my two-week-old niece. I haven't seen my big sister, Reeva in a long time; drugs make you stay away from people that love you the most. She looks like a flawless chocolate doll dressed in a beautiful pink dress, pink ruffles with pink panties underneath her dress, with some pink and white velcro barrettes, wrapped like a gift from Macy's secured in a hospital blanket. She's still and not making one peep. The precious doll began to cry. Reeva comes into the living room from the kitchen and slapped the taste out of Devin. "Get off of my baby!"

Reeva yells while she is as high as a kite preparing her exit. No one, in particular, was the designated sitter for this beautiful princess. Reeva sits in the chair, scratching as she nods off. "You're not going to lay around here all day and sleep," Queenie says to Reeva. Upset, Reeva storms out of the front door; she kicks the screen door, cursing and talking junk. "You always treat my mother's kids like trash! If my mother was here, you would not be acting like this!" Queenie yelled back, "Get out! I'm not having it. All yawl is crazy. On that stuff, girl, every eye closed ain't sleep. Ya stole my coins that I've been saving since 1918 and bought that stuff. I got some'den for ya! I got some'den for ya a**."

Someone Has to Pay — Rolita James

Can this day get any worse? My brother, Kahlil comes into the house and takes a deep sigh. He says, "I've joined the Army, I leave tonight," as he hung his head, slowly raising it staring at the ceiling. Silence filled the room. Before a word was said, there was a knock on the door. Kahlil goes to the screen door. "Yes, may I help you," he says to the white woman dressed in her cigarette ash grey suit. "Good afternoon; I am looking for Ms. Queenie." With tears welling up in her eyes, Queenie goes to the door. "May I help you?" "Hi Ms. Queenie, my name is Mrs. Carol Banks. I've spoken with you about Jacy, her unfortunate mishaps, and her behavior. This will be a great opportunity to place Jacy in a better environment. I'm with Bridging the Gap Juvenile Detention Home."

"Ok." Queenie softly replies. "I hope this turns her around because if it doesn't, her behavior will be her ruin. I don't know. I just don't know about these kids. I tried to give them a nice life and keep them all together. Ruby promised Reeva a car if she would just finish High School. She wouldn't even do that. On that stuff! I'm old; I had this little Xena since she was four and a half years old." Shaking her head as she takes a deep breath, she heads toward the kitchen and begins to wipe down the already

Someone Has to Pay   Rolita James

cleaned counter. Everybody in the house is crying, including Devin and the cigarette ash grey suit lady. Jacy holds on to the screen door grinding her teeth as the tears roll down her face dripping on her orange shirt. There are two things our family is very familiar with: Pain and Anger. Can you relate?

    With all that going on, Carol, who is Megan's aunt on her father's side, came strolling in with her fine silky black hair, fair skin-okay, high yellow, did I mention very loud self? Carol looks Cape Verdean or something. She's an undercover lush. She came to pick Megan up to bring her to Vermont. Carol always had a lot of kids around her. This doesn't look like a day or even a weekend trip. Megan comes over and wipes Denim's soaked chin and clears my eyes with her thumb, and says she will be back to see us.

    It's now dusk and Devin has to go home. I am so broken and hurt and I feel so lost. The atmosphere is very eerie. It's dinner time. No one has an appetite except Devin. He will leave after he eats fried chicken, rice topped with butter, sweet corn on the cob, and a warm, soft homemade dinner roll from Queenie's gangsta friend, Miss. Ida, with a cup of Kool-Aid. Devin uses our house to escape his abusive father's drinking; knowing that his father will jump on him while his mother acts as if she doesn't see it nor hear her son getting the crap beat out of him. She knows if she chimes in Johnny Walker will start counting to find her too. They live in North Stamford. Who would have thought?

The dishes were all cleaned up. We sold the last twenty Cherry, Grape, Orange, and Lime Icy's within twenty minutes. Turned on the TV, the highlight of the day was *Good Times*. Although JJ Evan's family is jacked up, they seem to survive. I can't relate. I am staring at the floor model television with a thousand questions racing through my mind. How did we get here? Are they going to be alright? How can I fix this situation and get everybody back home? "Dy-no-mite!" is not funny this night. I can't help but worry about my sisters and my brother. Reeva comes back still high to get Princess and take her home to a project complex. Being from the projects, you know the rules: don't cry over spilled milk, adjust and move on. Even if you're dying inside, people of color could not afford counseling, so we lived for over 400 years without and were told to get over it and stop being so angry. Start the day with God and prayer, and we end the day with

God and prayer. To think this was all in one day. Now here I am in my room on my knees for prayer. The Lord's Prayer is a must. God, do I thank you for this day? I have a question.

Chapter 3

A Way to Make It

"Lord, give me strength"

This right here is a game-changer. The life, the lessons, and the legacy of this amazing woman would produce preparation for victories, failures, and everyday life structure. The tools that she put into my, I call it, "A Way to Make It toolbox," Man oh man! I believe that this was my saving grace for having my first child at twenty years old and being a blessing by opening my home. For my marriage, my toolbox assisted me in dealing with love language conflicts within, going to counseling after four of my sisters passed away young, reading the whole book about a person instead of judging a book by the cover or reading one chapter of a person's life and assuming falsified information as fact. My toolbox came in handy even down to being an entrepreneur, a philanthropist, and preparing a loving environment for my HIV, heroin-addicted, stealing family members along with abandoned and rejected homeless people.

When it came to a way, she said there is always one. Those were Queenie's words. This saying was a blessing and a curse - A blessing because it taught me to survive and my troubles didn't always last. Excuse me as I pause for a moment of gratitude. I'll get back to the blessings in a minute.

Queenie took guardianship of me after losing my mother, her firstborn to giving herself an abortion for the twins that she was carrying. I watched her make a way and take care of my mother's six children; however, the strength of her story didn't start here. Whew! Having her own mother, Utica passed away while she was at a tender young age, being separated from her three other siblings for a while, and being raised by a mean Aunt were all a part of Queenie's story. At five years old, she had to walk for miles alone to go to school, walking by swamps, hearing the sound of snakes through the tall fields of cotton. Can you imagine being five years old and terrified but still walking to school every day? Not only did she have to watch out for the snakes in the tall grass, but she also had to hide from the white men on horses too. Back in those days, and I suppose in these days as well, there was no telling what could happen to a little Black girl traveling by herself. Queenie dropped out of school at nine years old to work for a white family that just had a baby. She told me about cooking her first meal for this family; she said she made string beans, rice, and burnt fried chicken. Burnt on the outside and not fully cooked on the inside; even burning herself by the pop of hot grease didn't stop her from doing it again to get it right. She made a way and kept trying until she perfected it. A testament to who she was.

One of her daughters was kidnapped; it ripped her apart. She was reunited with her at forty. Her daughter called her when she was a young lady and said that she heard about her and she wanted to come and live with her mother. At that time, she already had the six of us plus a few others in a two-bedroom, so she did what she thought was right and said to her, "I'm going to try to get more space so that you can come." Now that may have been her way of "making a way," but her daughter felt as if her mother was rejecting her. She felt as if her mother didn't want her because she was willing to sleep in a tub just to be with her mother. I guess only God knows the kingdom turn out. Both of them made pure decisions from a painful unclear place.

Pausing with tears in my eyes I wonder how many of us have had to do some things in life over until we've perfected them. Still, the first time around, we burnt it; whether it was in a marriage, relationship, parenting, a job, getting our first credit card, religion, your first perm, starting your first business, having sex, cutting your hair, shaving, learning to drive, even singing your first solo in the Church choir? Wheww! That made me think of Jerry Johnson, who sang in the choir. Whatever happened to him?

One thing I knew for sure was when it came to problem-solving - there's a way!

Now for the curse, I believed that if it was meant to be that it was up to me in the universe (curse) blinded by this phrase, I've even jeopardized the well-being of my family by taking in numerous homeless relatives and men and women from the streets. Some had mental issues, health issues, criminal records, unhealthy pasts with substance abuse, and even poor communication. I thought that if I "made a way," they would somehow be ok. If I took them into my home and gave them food, water, clothes, a shower, a place to sleep and love, maybe just maybe things would turn around for them. My son gave up his living quarters all of the time. I felt their struggle. Does that sound familiar?

Our home was broken into three times (curse), rape (curse), no one helped out financially (curse), someone told me that they could take my husband from me; they had been in my house for about 2 1/2- 3 years (curse), a homeless man told me how sexy I was as I walked to the bathroom in the dark (curse), guns found under my son's bed from the FBI (curse), giving a homeless person all new stuff to survive to have it all destroyed the next day. Those all seemed like curses to me.

To sum it up and describe this precious gem of a Grandmother of mine. She was strong, very loyal, committed, and religious. She was an entrepreneur who owned a daycare and sold icy's. Queenie had jokes for days; she understood the struggle, she was quiet, and she planted a peach tree in the hood that fed people for years. Bowling was her harmony, and God was the foundation of her life.

This saying, "a way to make it," demonstrated by Queenie's life has my toolbox full of fantastic learning tools that have built me into the strong woman I am today. Queenie made a way. She taught me how to make one too. There's no doubt that the impact she had on my life saved my life in more than one way. She paved the way, paid the price, and made a way for me, for all of us. Queenie was a queen indeed.

Chapter 4

Reggie

"You'll eat it before it eats you."

I want to ask you a question. Is it possible that a Cocaine snorting, club-hopping, gun-totting, fork rat-stabbing, NYC street running, and music promoting man could have been an angel in disguise?

While making my success moves without instructions or coaching, I went back and forth to New York to do skits and plays for money. I didn't have a good relationship with finances, I knew to save some, but I never had much of it, so saving $100 dollars was a big deal. While walking down the streets of New York City with undeniable confidence, I met this tall, light-skinned, dominating, and so debonair man named Reggie. I was ignorant on fire; imagine the flames. So we began having this mind-orgasmic conversation. I told you that I was mature for my age, a self-proclaimed writer, a self-proclaimed director, a member of a renowned rap group, and a self-proclaimed professional dancer. I could dance better than most of my peers did, so that makes me a professional? Oh well, as I was saying, I self-proclaimed myself. I was also a self-proclaimed model because I did a few fashion shows with big names in the industry, and I even made one magazine. With all of my credentials I had it made, I was the one for Reg. Hanging out with him was electrifying. See coming from Stamford, Connecticut, having a lot of siblings that had a lot of friends, being in a gang, Queenie having a daycare, going to Bible Study in my hood with Mother Gingiddy she taught us this at the end of every Bible Study:

"I HAVE TO LIVE WITH MYSELF AND SOUL. I WANNA BE FIT FOR MYSELF TO KNOW. I

WANNA BE ABLE, AS THE DAY GOES BY, TO ALWAYS LOOK MYSELF STRAIGHT IN THE EYE, I DON'T WANT TO STAND WITH THE SADDEST SON AND HATE MYSELF FOR THE THINGS I'VE DONE AMEN."

This was something I never forgot. I even went to the most prominent Baptist Church in the city. What is my point on the in-between? I wasn't successful; I was just popular.

Spending quality time with Reggie I quickly found out that all that I was in Connecticut meant nothing, nor did it have any merit in the Bronx where Reggie was from or in Manhattan, New York. Without Reggie, no one even knew that I existed. Every moment was an adventure. Six-inch stilettos hitting the concrete jungle from club to club, record to record, room to room and sniff to sniff. My adrenaline racing as my heart pounded with the subsequent encounter, an episode of what I would like to call a "field trip" with Reg. Always educational, good or bad.

When it came to making love or having sex, I shared with Reggie my desire to wait until I was married. He didn't force the issue. In fact, from the look in his eyes and his behavior, it appeared that he respected me for not getting high, drinking, or being like other women that he had experienced. I mean, being that fine, I'm sure he had already had more than enough of his share of red lights, ceilings with nets, zodiac posters, wet ones, and dry ones. Yet, he kept me around and introduced me to his world.

Fast forward one day, Reggie picked me up from the Fordham Road Train Station. We stopped by a new club, grabbed a bite to eat then were en route to his place. Reggie got comfortable taking all of his clothes off and getting in the bed seductively inviting me. Being on top of my game, I thought to myself; I know what this is! He is testing me! After showing me some of the most intense exposure to the underground life, Reg wants to see if I will be loyal to him. Know that a man needs love, support, loyalty, and sex. In case my assumption was valid, I slowly slid my clothes off, glancing at him, his gun on the nightstand and the door thinking he had already called a goon to off me, put cement on my feet, and dump me near the Statue of Liberty. Oh my, I'm finito. Someone was going to burst in and shoot me, paranoid from all that I have seen. I was telling myself, oh s%*#^ I'm in too deep! I got in the bed and laid next to Reggie. He held me close, it felt almost magical. He looked at me intently, and said, "You are so beautiful with your amazing eyes. They make me want to change." I could feel his skin becoming one with mine, the sound of his voice commanding the atmosphere, placing his finger of power on my forehead slowly caressing my face, there is a pause, and he says, "Get dressed, I'm going to take you somewhere." Once again, back on a roller coaster, I'm hyped, excited, cautious, and having my life flash before me. Shy, I grab the sheets and the covers to go to the bathroom to get dressed, hearing the sound of Reggie chuckle. "Really love?"

I get dressed, and I hear what sounds like he is picking up his gun and jewelry. I quickly remembered one night we went into the back of a backroom. Reg was eating, and a rat came strolling across the table. Reggie stabbed the rat with his fork and went back to eating. I had my hands on his shoulder while he ate. When he

Someone Has to Pay   Rolita James

stabbed the rat and went back to eating, I had to think fast and didn't want anyone in that circle to question my toughness. I was cringing, cursing, and screaming inside. What the hell! I checked the bathroom window to see how far down I would have to jump to get away and if he had pit bulls ready to eat me like I was a piece of raw steak. Reggie knocked on the bathroom door; I jumped and broke out in a sweat. "Love, are you ready?" I say yes, I'll be right out. I grab the toothpaste because I would gauge his eye out with the end of the tube if he tried anything. As I opened the door slowly, Reggie was putting his belt on, standing looking in the mirror sexy as hell. What an incredible 6'4 piece of eye candy.

He was extending his hand for me to place my palm into his. He walks me to the car, opens my door, puts my seatbelt on, closes and locks my side, and walks around to the driver's side. He then gets in the car, makes all the adjustments, and we head off.

We are on the highway. Reggie holds my hand; all is well. He looks at me. I look at him with joy and tell him how amazing today was. I turn to look out of the window and realize that we are heading I-95 North. I assume he is pulling out the romantic side of him, showing me another side that I haven't seen. I'm now considering maybe I will make love to him with great anticipation of the night and shining armor fantasy. I am so caught up in the world that I created that when I came back to reality, I was at 25 Tillman Place Stamford, CT. Reggie came to the passenger side, opened the door, took my hand, kissed me on my forehead as a sign of maximum respect and said. "Love - God has something more significant for you." He turned and walked away and drove off, never to be seen again.

REGGIE #2

I had had some very crucial moments in my life, and this particular season was one of them. I went to Norfolk, Virginia to visit a friend because my marriage at the time was falling apart without a clear explanation; at least from my frame of reference. It was cold, snowing, and time to go back to an unhappy checked-out husband. Due to the inclement weather, I decided to wear my Candy Apple red comfortable sweatsuit with my Hillary Clinton hairdo, neither of which has ever let me down before. One day while wearing my famous sweatsuit, this guy from Winston-Salem, NC said to me, "Wow! You are so pretty, looking all delicious in that sweatsuit, looking like a caramel candy apple!" So me and my Candy Apple red sweatsuit that never offended anyone headed to the airport. I make it to my gate. I began reading a book when this very distinguished gentleman is sitting across from me wearing a dark suit with a charcoal grey long-length cashmere overcoat and scarf; he was sharp. He leans forward with a look of interest and says, "Hello - What is the name of the book that you're reading?" I showed him it was

"The Power of a Praying Wife." I decided to share my dilemma because I had never seen him in my life, so what did I have to lose? Over the intercom, an announcement is made that we have a three-hour delay. Ughhhhh! While fighting for my marriage and going through undiagnosed depression, happy helping others, and then eating and going straight to bed so that I wouldn't be in anyone's way, my confidence had gone down a few notches. Now I'm even a little self-conscious of my big Candy Apple Sweatsuit. He asked my name. I said, "Xena. Xena

Smith." Then I say, "your name Sir?" He responds, "Reggie." My eyes are wide open.

We spent the next three hours sharing stories. Reggie worked for the NBA at Madison Square Garden. Three hours passed, and they finally called for all First Class travelers. Reggie says, "It was great speaking with you, Xena. They're calling me." I said, "Likewise, Reggie."

A voice over the intercom calls for all military, anyone with a disability, or small children with strollers. I started to walk up, but I changed my mind. I was still smiling, bubbly, and functioning even though I was in so much pain fighting for a lost cause, so I sat and waited for them to call my group.

"Now calling Groups 1 & 2, calling Groups 3 & 4, Groups 5 & 6, Calling 7 & 8. Final call for all groups." I get up, zoned out. I walk on the plane to see Reggie in the second seat, we smirk, and I look up to find my window seat, wait! Whaaaaaaaah! I'm in the last seat on the plane. "Excuse me, Ma'am. When I purchased my ticket, I selected a window seat." She smiles and says as politely as

Someone Has to Pay   Rolita James

she knew how. "Yes, the seat you're sitting in, although it has no window, it has a frame so it is considered a window seat. Consider yourself first class." I looked at her, offended. She assures me I will be the first to get my snack and drinks. I can't believe this!

Landing at Laguardia Airport, the bell goes off, you can hear all of the seat belts unlock, and everyone is getting off of the plane. That's right, you guessed it; I was the last on and the last to get off, but a pleasant surprise was waiting for me. Reggie was the first to get off the plane and patiently waited for me, the last one to get off the plane. We walked together to baggage claim to get our luggage, and a Limousine driver was waiting with Reggie's First and last name. You could see the stretch Limo outside, parked at the curb.

Meanwhile, my husband comes in, doesn't speak to me, takes my luggage out of my hand, and turns and walks ahead of me. I'm trying to keep up thinking since he picked me up that meant that there was a chance that we would work things out, but he made it very clear that was not the case. Reggie began walking with his driver in the opposite direction. He turned around, and I heard a stern voice of confidence and strength. "Xena, Xena." I stopped in my tracks and turned around Reggie said, "You're beautiful, and you are worth much more than this." He turned and walked away, never to be seen nor heard from again.

Two angels named Reggie.

Chapter 5

Who Wants To Marry A Millionaire?

"Do you think money grows on trees?"

(Ring)
Me: "Hello."
Guy: "Good evening! May I speak with Xena?"
Me: "This is her, who's dis?"
Guy: "Cortez from the learning center where you work."
Me: "Oh! Hey! What's up?"

Cortez: "I heard that you are very popular and do a lot of things in the community. I was wondering if you and I can meet up because the learning center is having a big concert and will be bringing in a few celebrities. I would like it very much if you can help us with promoting this particular event."

Me: "Ok - no prob."

Cortez: "How's this Friday?"

Me: "I can't! I'm going to a prom."

Cortez: "Oh, Wow! Stop by the center so your co-workers can see you."

Me: "Cool! See you lata, have a good night."

Fast forward to Friday.

The door opens to the black stretch Limousine. Shoe one hits the ground of the learning center parking lot. Boom! Shoe two hits the ground. I can see the cameras flashing, the red carpet rolled out, hear the cheers and applause from the crowd of people that don't exist. Wow, it's all in my head. I'm still cheesing hard, as my cream, form-fitting gown clings to my high, big booty - yet slim, Hershey's. Walking into the learning center yelling, "Hey y'all!"

Cortez, who doesn't mingle with the employees, comes out of his office and our eyes lock for the first time. In my mind, I'm like, wait! I know this clown. He's the guy that threw up all over his baseball jacket at my brother's party. Are you kidding me? Nasty self! I can hear the whisper in this sexy tone (Dayummm) as he bites his lip. Being popular, I acted as if I didn't just see his look or hear it. Well, I'm about to head out. I exited the stage and left.

Back to work at the learning center on Monday, to my surprise, Cortez is there.

Cortez: "Xena, do you have a minute?"

As I continue putting away books,
Me: "Sure! What's up?"

Cortez: "Well! I was going to give out flyers in the community today; I was wondering if I let you off work a little earlier would you go with me?"
Me: "Sure, no problem. I got chu!"

"Great!" He says. We get off work, hop in his Black on Black Convertible Mustang and start heading toward my hood, aka project complex. We walk behind one of the buildings where it is chained so no cars can go through the backway if the police are chasing them plus, I couldn't be seen with this clean-cut dork, so I speed up a little. It sounds like someone got punched in the stomach. I freeze and slowly turn around. It felt like it took me forever to find Cortez on the ground. He was viewing the flyer for errors, didn't notice the chain, walked smack into it, and flipped over it. I ran laughing so hard and loud my side was hurting. His arms were stretched out, his glasses were half off of his face as he looked dazed into the sky. I had to calm myself down. I got on my knees, put one hand under his head and one hand on his chest. "Cortez, are you ok? Can you hear me?" Trying not to burst out laughing, he whispers "Yeah." I'm like, what happened again now and burst out laughing. "Ok, ok, ok, please forgive me. Didn't you see that big ass chain? Making sure that you're ok is more important. Lay here for a minute. I will hold you."

Cortez whispered, but I couldn't quite make out what he said as I saw the flyers blowing through the air in the back of the building. I bent my head down a little more to his mouth so that I could hear, Wait! Why do I see stars as his tongue goes in my mouth and he caresses my hair? I tilt my head, slowly suck his bottom lip for five seconds, and send his body into a hood trance. Oh my! Now I'm saying what he said the day he saw me going to the prom (Dayummmm), I say in my mind.

We are from two different worlds, Two different sides of town with two words that were bringing us together as one; hot and heavy. This chemistry is off of the radar. Everything in my body was at attention to his command without him knowing. Cortez knows nothing about the hood. He's not supposed to be here. He slowly glides his lips across my cheek to my ear and says, "Are you sure you're ready for this ride? I want you to be mine."

"Don't worry about the flyers; I'll make more."

Cortez and I have been together now for almost two years, and He is still sneaking into my hood. Let me just say, his mother is an ambassador for the embassy, and his father is an OBGYN so you can understand how different our worlds are. One beautiful day he calls me extremely upset asking if I was available.

He said, "I'm coming to pick you up now." Without a chance to answer, I prepare for his arrival. He drives towards the Hutchinson parkway. The scene is breathtaking. "What's wrong?" I ask. "Nothing," he says. However, I can tell that something has him upset, because his jawbone was tight while protruding. Pulling into a mall parking lot, Cortez comes over to my side to open the door. I get out of the car, he pulls me close to him and says, "Xena, I feel so safe with you, I can be 100% me; you are the most authentic person that I have ever met in my life." (A Hood tendency) "Ok." I respond.

We go to the mall, and again I'm a little ahead of him. He starts trying to grope me, flirting. I yell, "Cortez! Stop! I'm not playing with you!" Then, I take off running. Here he comes, running behind me and laughing, so I scream to embarrass him, and he turns to walk away. Now I'm chasing him. I catch him and jump on his back for a piggyback ride hoping that it eases the anger; it does. He says, "Xena, do you want something to eat?" knowing that food is a comforter. We set out to grab a bite, and I say, "Cortez, what are we going to do for our second anniversary?" His answer was head slanting worthy.

Cortez: "Have my parents stop knowing every freaking move I make. I believe that they pay someone to follow me. Xena, they told me every place that we've ever eaten, every single time I came to your house, other outings. The way I laugh when I'm with you." My mom said, "I don't see what you see in that little short girl from the ghetto.'"

Now hold on. Did I share with you that back in the day, Cortez's mother was my Girl Scout instructor? When I was younger, she told me that I could be whatever I wanted to be when I grew up. Did I tell you that Cortez and his family owned the learning center where I worked? She hired me because she saw way back then that I was cut from a different cloth. Things hit different when it's close to home. Ok, I will sit that right here.

On our Second Anniversary, we are at the beach one beautiful June day; the waves are clashing against the stones, sometime after dusk. The perfect mood for our Second Anniversary. We are walking on the pier holding hands, laughing; he appears so free. Chemistry is still as high as it was when he flipped over the chain. We now have our blanket spread out in the sand with our shoes parked next to the blanket, laid out relaxing and talking.

I run to the car to grab a picnic basket. He is so surprised and appreciative, smiling from ear to ear, not caring if his parents knew where he is, who he was with, or even what he was doing. He rolls over on top of me and begins to kiss my neck, whispering Happy Anniversary.

Cortez: "Xena Baby. I've been waiting for this Mmmmm. This beach will never be the same, after today I should buy this beach for you. You deserve it! Thank you for making me feel safe when I'm with you. (sucking on my breast) Xena thank you for making me laugh, holding my secrets. (coming up for air) Not judging me, (our lips connecting as he pauses and looks me in my eyes) You are so beautiful!"

As he lay between my legs, I roll over on him to share how happy I am that it was our anniversary. Let's just say if we were in the room, it would be LIGHTS OUT. You guys are so nosey. Ha! As we packed the car up, Cortez looked at me, and said, "I have to tell you something." I look at him with a secure look. I'm from the hood we believe that we can handle anything. I reached for his hand, and assure him it's always going to be honest with us, you can tell me anything. He grabs my hair, kisses me, looks me dead in my eyes, and says, "I just got you pregnant with the most beautiful baby boy ever. You won't ever have to worry about anything; he will be taken care of. I want you to be my wife."

(Fast forward four months later)

I'm at work, I am so happy, I am feeling great, I haven't had any morning sickness and haven't gained a pound.

Cortez: "Xena I told my mom, she is not happy, she wished that I was married, she is pissed, but if she gets quiet around you, just ignore it. I say, "Ok, I got you." Cortez confidently says, "I gave her a card to read while I'm at work, and it will give her some time to cool off." (High five!)

His mother is surprisingly pleasant and very friendly to me, and I'm going into my fifth month. One day the janitor was cleaning the learning center and mopped the floor with Ammonia and Bleach mixed. Whelp! I couldn't take it and became very ill. After all of the appointments, everyone has left the office building, I couldn't take anymore, and I had to go.

Cortez's mother called to ask how I was feeling. I said, "Ma'am, that ammonia and bleach were very strong, and it got the baby very sick." "Excuse me!!" she exclaimed. In a very assertive tone she said, "Xena, you can stay home." Still trusting Cortez with my whole heart I say, "Oh, thank you so much, Ma'am. I will be in tomorrow." Her response took me for another loop.

"No, you won't be in tomorrow or any other day!"

Phone drops. It hit me like a ton of bricks Cortez's mother didn't know. Confused and now afraid, I'm home thinking, what am I going to do? No worries, he said that we would be ok. He will give us the world. I will be married to a millionaire that is crazy in love with me.

(Ring)

Me: "Hello."

Cortez: "Hey."

Me: "What's going on? Your mother didn't know I was pregnant. She found out today. She fired me!

Cortez: Quiet.

Me: "How am I supposed to help take care of our child? I know that you guys own five learning centers and the football stadium, but I want to help. I have your back forever."

Cortez: Still quiet.

Me: "Cortez, what are you thinking?"

Cortez: "My mom called me in a meeting with my father and said that she would not have any ghetto grandchild in her family from no ghetto chic with nothing going for herself and will never be anything. Xena, You have to have an abortion."

Me: "Five months pregnant, Cortez? Really? Who does that? Come over. Let's go to our safe place. I need to feel safe now."

Cortez: "I'm coming over to give you some money for the abortion. I looked it up; it's five hundred dollars at the clinic."

Me: "I don't have that kind of money."

Cortez: "I'm on my way; meet me outside."

I meet him outside, and he gives me seventy-five dollars towards the five hundred dollars and tells me to figure something out knowing good and doggone well that I don't have that kind of money.

Cortez: "I made the appointment for you for tomorrow, but I didn't tell them how far along you were, so don't tell them. Tell them that you are eight weeks, not five months."

Someone shake me. My perfect reality had taken a turn to another reality.

(Phone ring)

Me: "Hello."

Cortez: "Hey Xena. How are you feeling?"

Me: "How should I be feeling?"

Cortez: "Did you take care of that today?"

Me: "Yes."

Cortez: "Great! Whew! That was close."

Me: "What was close?"

Cortez: "My parents said that I had to choose, the will of millions of dollars or a kid from the projects and don't be stupid. (Pause) I chose the will. They said to have the millions, I have to sever all ties with you."

Me: "So, you just gave me $75.00 and you walk?"

Cortez: "Xena! Don't do this. I wash my hands."

Me: "Cortez! You are washing your hands in the mud."

Just like that our perfect real world had been shattered for millions as if it never existed. He didn't see our son until he was ten years old.

Who paid? Someone or everyone?

Chapter 6

When Everybody Loves You But Me

*"**Nobody wants to be loved for what they got, but for who they are.**"*

Happened

Massive confusion, emotions chaotic, silence is painful, heartache . . . crucial.

As time passed

What are the signs, how will I know? With all that's entangled, what is the flow? Why do I keep falling for the? Pretenders that give off the impression that it's secure and all is well.

As time passed

I'm getting fed up with myself, fed up with my choosing you to be my leading companion and I'm 2** star rated when I give my best. Oh, I get it. Just because I don't know when it happened doesn't mean I don't know what happened.

It all made sense in my world; influenced by my tunnel vision, I thought I had it all figured out. I never even gave it a second thought. You know that feeling when you know that you know, that you know? Do you know that universal mindset of love? I'm talking about the perfect happiness kind of love, amazing sex kind of love, great paying jobs kind of love, raising children together kind of love, that everybody loves the family pet kind of love, nice cars in the driveway kind of love, ice cream sundae with the cherry on the top kind of love? Of course, you can't have the "American Dream" without the white picket fence kind of love.

Going with my heart this time went against my physical appetite, yet he unintentionally prophesied me into our future. Even though he wasn't my type, he proclaimed me as his wife before he even truly knew me, and I became his wife; that's how powerful words are. You should know that is the power of the spoken word.

The way we laughed, the way we played, the way we talked on the phone all night even as we dozed off, no one wanting to hang up first. Giving all of myself, withholding nothing, only to have some people say, "You're the best, I love you." and at the same time be unwanted and called the worst by others. Has anyone besides me been there before? I remember one time he even walked across town because he heard the love of his life, who never had a drink in her life, was drunk. He met me slumped with my pants open on the bench after drinking five different kinds of liquor, trying to hang with my siblings and cousins who were veterans in that rodeo. One time one of the "he's" pulled out a gun and put it to my head, calling it a deeper connection. I'm not sure what he intended to do, but I do believe God sent his mother home from work early sick that day because it simply wasn't my time to die. Another "he" taught me how to drive by having me sit on his lap and then went on the highway, forcing me to drive and making it clear that he was ready to die if that's what happened. Can you believe that? In all that craziness, it still wasn't my time to leave here either.

They would do anything to be in my presence, I made them feel like Kings, and they said I was the best thing that ever happened to them, and as a result, through the years, they would call me for encouragement or just to laugh. One day thirty years later, I was out of the country and found out they committed suicide. (If you or someone you know is suicidal, having mental health challenges, depression, or negative thoughts, it is real and serious. Please get some help at the National Suicide Prevention Lifeline at 800-273-8255.) I'm aware that it was not my fault, yet it didn't change the pain of the loss. I suppose there are a few ways to lose your grip on love, even down to letting your own grip loose regardless of how much you want to hold it tight.

He thought because I was popular and known by most that I wasn't pure. He didn't realize I had fourteen siblings, a close-knit family was multi-talented: from learning how to cornrow, dance, fight, color guard, model, write plays, rap, moving from hood to hood, to Queenie being the Icy Lady in the projects, and living as a natural-born leader; these were all contributions to my popularity. Plus, just so we're clear, love-making was NOT up for discussion when Queenie was raising you. Her sayings about the sex matter: (If you can't define it, you shouldn't be doing it) Just keep your legs clean and closed. That's it, That's all—end of discussion.

One day I went to the Avenue pure; they called me over to the porch. We were hanging out. They asked me if I wanted some water, and I said sure, as we went inside our mutual friend's house. A generational barrier muted me. I had no idea that love and making love was something to be discussed, but regardless of my ignorance, the encounter was a transfer of information. No longer in possession of the purity, I came to the Avenue with, that sexual experience that looked like a massacre, and when we were done, they kissed my face thinking the moisture was sweat. They looked down at me to wipe what they thought was sweat away from our faces and realized it was blood and tears—jumping up, looking for something to wipe my face and their lips, only to notice the blood on the walls and floor. Guilt and sorrow set in with the words ringing, "I'm so sorry, I didn't know. I thought you were open. I'm sorry." (Pause) "You're all mine now."

I stayed on mute and ran home. I sat in the tub for hours trying to process what just happened. Ignorance and silence robbed me of that precious moment.

Wait!! Now I'm in a full-blown relationship, not knowing they didn't truly want me? They were a pro and a self-proclaimed ones at that. Strolling in "my introduction to an intimate relationship" High School hallway only to hear sexual sounds. As I snooped, I found them screwing another girl and the nerve of them telling me that I will always love them because they were my first.

Wow! I'm alive. I recognize all along it was God's hand, Queenie's prayers, and someone that I don't know; burdens to stand in the gap and feel my struggles. Yup! Singing: "Somebody prayed for me, had me on their mind, took the time to pray for me. I'm so glad they prayed for me." Aye!

Someone Has to Pay — Rolita James

I have to lift my hands and heart with much adoration. Every single time I found something to cling onto, I called that thing perfect even though there were many other things that I've done to myself or allowed to share my space that was actually toxic. I didn't give it a name at the time, even the consequences of some were fatal, yet I felt they were deserving. Giving yourself the answers without wisdom, life's education, blinders on, and generational limitations can jack you up! Loving people with the fantasy that they will love you back, believing everyone grows up with the same definition of love, deep affection, and intense feeling for someone or something can do a number on not only you but your own perception of yourself. I had no clue that love had a vernacular. Even though you have a primary language, it's great to be bilingual to accommodate the attraction of the one that you say you Love. In giving everyone a piece of me in one way or another, the remnant wanted to be loved with an honest tongue, sincere heart, and full accessibility. You see, I was living to survive once again. Who was loved in this chapter? I thought everyone loved me. How, when I didn't even love myself? During these times, I didn't have any standards, deal-breakers, or information. Ask yourself about you wanting others to love you even when they are emotionally unavailable. Do you want to participate in the way they love? If so, how? love is a language. Love is a choice - choose wisely and do it freely. As for me, I'm living for love and purpose alone. I chose to abide in love. Are you Abiding in love? (input) a Rose

Chapter 7

Promises, Promises

"Just because you ain't know, don't mean it ain't so"

"I promise you when I see you, imma drop you on sight." I said it, and I meant it. I had no idea that the promise I made three years earlier would be why I was making the promise that just left my lips. Yeah, sometimes one thing can indeed lead to another. It makes me think of when promises are made, why promises are broken, and who intends to keep them or break them. Sometimes the intent doesn't even matter because we all know about good intentions too. I certainly had no idea the same promise would be broken, but I guess that's the risk in promise. Whether it's calculated or not, the risk is there. I've heard the saying promises are meant to be broken. I don't believe that to be true, but I've seen my share of broken promises and the shattered expectations they leave behind; the residue, the evidence of fragmented hope, eventually overcome with disappointment.

I wonder, once a promise is broken, can it ever be repaired? Can the fractured thing be mended, or is the break forever and a new guarantee made? Is one promise worth the risk of another? Was the promise to be supportive worth the support I once knew being taken from me? The Word says count up the cost.

Helping is a part of my makeup, so I extended the support when I saw a woman in a less-than-ideal situation. When I said, "If you need anything, call me." It was a promise to help a person in need. I didn't have anything and everything in mind, but a promise is a promise. I'm not sure if people think about promises. Big or small. How many promises have you not kept? How many have you broken? How many times did you think the promise meant something that it actually didn't? The thing about promises is everybody's walking around speaking a different language. Making promises in their own language and breaking them in another one. In the end, people walk away with two different versions of hurt, two different stories of how another failed to keep their word. Life has taught me, that it's not common to be on the same page. A lot of times, we complain about the promises that weren't kept to us. What about the ones we rob ourselves of through thought, word, or deed?

Now here I am, promising. Case in point: a few months later, the eight-month pregnant, messy-haired woman I told to call me if she needed me, asked me for what she needed. I ended up babysitting her newborn a few times a week. That overnight led to her moving into my house for a few years. This promise, although not what I had in mind, I didn't mind in the ways I thought I would. She had a need, and I promised I would help her if she called. What started as a need for a babysitter turned into a need for a place to stay. I didn't know necessity would extend itself to my husband. This promise had me sleeping on the couch instead of in the bed with my husband. I didn't find out right away, but a promise of love and to be faithful ended up being just another fractured agreement. A covenant unkept.

In retrospect, it wasn't something that I had ever expected to happen. At least not like the way it did. I had made a promise to love, and I meant that. I even loved when I didn't necessarily feel loved, but that's what a promise is. It's a declaration, its assurance of a particular outcome. People had taken advantage of me in other ways but not ever like this. That's how one promise can lead to the breaking of others.

The issue is people don't have the same commitment; people don't have the same plan. I promised to love my husband till death do we part, and we got divorced. God had His own plan too. He's the only true promise keeper.

As I sat in the pulpit getting ready to preach, I heard the Lord say, "promises will be broken." What didn't make sense to me at that moment would shortly. Not too long after, I saw the woman I had promised to help if she needed anything. I saw her and the string of contract breeching that came along with the promise I had made. The last thing I had promised her was to drop her on sight if I saw her. I can look back and laugh, but that promise was broken too.

It makes me think about the promises of God and when they collide with the reality of our expectations. What happens when it doesn't add up to us? When we weren't in the room where other promises were made, but the contractual agreements of them shift and shake our lives. When we didn't see it coming? The reason why there is no court case is because it isn't an accident. When we don't see the changes, it doesn't mean things are still the same. Patterns are the perquisites to promise. People in our lives could change and act differently because we ignore the patterns. The making, breaking, and sustaining of a promise is the sum total of a pattern. What did you miss? What assumptions did you make? Those could be your most significant missteps that could change everything. Did you follow your gut? Follow your gut.

What I know to be true is God has promises for my life. Some have been realized, and some have yet to manifest. I shut the stage in Las Vegas down after the promise of it looking bleak at a time when I wasn't sure if I would be able to speak again. I went on to do the very things others couldn't promise me and started making better promises to myself, ones that I could keep. Ones that I will keep. I'm not here to be liked, but I promise I will be remembered.

The only thing that's a promise is that God will love us forever. Promises, Promises.

I cheated; he cheated. No one held their end of the bargain. How did we get here? Divorce.

Someone told me I was the girl of their dreams. They had wanted me since 2010. They were pursuing me the whole time, and I decided to give them a commitment only to learn they were cheating the entire time; a baby came from the cheating. Promises broken, dreams shattered, hope lost, truth charcoaled. I went back into an emotional hole of disappointment.

In the reading of this book, did you notice that all of my siblings were drug addicts with very heavy hearts for different reasons? They're all dead. I promised myself I would never do drugs, even prescription drugs. You can count me out. To God be the Glory! I kept the promise by God's grace. You see if you've ever been an addict to anything- drugs, sex, alcohol, food, strange habits, eating boogers, toxicity-you get the point; then you know it's only by God's grace one can be delivered. I want your gut check wheels to turn.

Examine yourself. I can't tell you what it does to your body. I can talk about what it does to your family. I can tell you that Your kids might be adjusting to calling someone else mom and dad. We are eating a good dinner while you're out on the corner eating a bodega sandwich by yourself, and the food is good, but you're not there. You promised to be back, but your seat is empty at the table because you don't want anyone to say anything, and the whole time you're not considering how your family feels looking at your empty spot as they chew. Addictions make you selfish. I remember I promised my sister I would take her kids. She said, promise me that if anything happens to me, you will take my kids. We were only a year apart. Her husband was abusive and infected her with HIV. One day I went to visit; my instinct told me to bring my gun.

As we were in bed talking, we eventually fell asleep. Being a light sleeper, I heard him growling, standing over my sister with a bat in his hands. I put my fingers to my lip and backed him out of the room. AIDS killed him before I did, not knowing two years later she would be gone too and I would have to adopt her daughters.

Another promise that I've made and kept is to live my passion, what's in my heart. Live full and die empty, travel the world, and help. Only work doing what I love. How are you living your life in freedom? Are you doing what you love without hurting others? What great promises have you made to yourself? How's that working out for you? Please head in that direction if you're all over the place, in a dead-end job or at a job that you hate, in an unfulfilling relationship, or ignorant about other races.

Sometimes the storm comes to clear your path. The road is clear.

I heard someone say to a female, "I love you," and she said, "I love you too." She smiled, blew a kiss, and left. I said to the guy, "Wait, I didn't know you loved her." His response was that his love for her was Universal, and the definition and emotion are left to the interpreter. How's that for an interpretation?

Chapter 8

University of hard knocks

"A hard head makes a soft behind"

I remember when the white lady knocked on our door, and Kahlil answered. It was a woman coming to tell Queenie that Jacy would be better in a home. I remember the pain on Queenie's face that day. I remember that knock of news that shook our world back then. I was too little to recollect everything, but I remember the look of sadness on Queenie's face. A look you could feel, and I felt it that day.

Someone Has to Pay   Rolita James

I want to ask, did you hear the knock at your door? I think about all the times I listened to a knock. The times the knock made me excited, the times it made me nervous, the times it made me anxious, the times it produced no response in me at all; just made me tell somebody else to get it.

Every knock is not the same. A Postal service knock is different from the knock of your children. A knock of confidence is not the same knock as doubt. The knock of the gift giver is not the same as the knock of a thief. What about the times we avoid the knock because no one wanted to face what was on the other side? It's funny how circumstances can dictate situations in life, how circumstance can make you feel prepared or not prepared for the knock, for what awaits on the other side of the door, for the very thing that knocks.

I learned there are different types of doors and different types of knocks from Queenie. More importantly, I realized that what lies behind the other door on the inside is valuable. If something is knocking on you, you have to know you're valuable. The purpose is embedded in you because God breathed himself into you, and whatever is trying to get your attention knows that what's inside is great. That's why it's knocking.

I remember hearing a story about a young woman who had been raped, beaten, and left for dead in an alley. She was too weak to move, but she had a pulse. She looked left, no one in sight. She looked right and saw a lit cross in view. She had mustered the strength to crawl to the main street and found her way to a hospital after seeing the light. The lady staggered her way to the cross only to fall in the arms of a hospital security guard. That was the knock of purpose. In this case, the knock sounded like a heartbeat. The heartbeat was the knock. Your heartbeat is the knock. Bump. Bump. Bump. Those are knocks.

I learned that it might be a long road, but God will use somebody to be your miracle. It might look like it's over, but something still knocks on the inside of you where you refuse to give up.

There are quick knocks and slow knocks and knocks that sound and feel like contractions. Some knocks last a long time. Self-worth keeps knocking when you have low self-esteem. Have you ever heard the knock of worth, value, and prosperity? The knock of poverty was so loud, sounded like death was at the door sometimes.

You have to listen to the knock before you open up the door. Some knocks can get lost in the rhythm of life. You know the differences in the knocks. Knock of expectation or the knock of a plot. Some knocks sound like whispers, some might not even seem like knocks at all but all knocks teach you something.

The knock when something doesn't belong, the knocks you have to ignore, the knock when you have to separate yourself.

Can you hear a knock on a vault door? In a vault, you need a combination; there's one way and no knob on the inside because whatever is in there is meant to be in there. Only certain people have access to the vault. Whoever goes to the vault has to go with the leader. That's why people have to see themselves as winners because that's what gets you in the vault. Seeing yourself as victorious gives you access.

People open doors because they want to allow something to come. People open doors because they want to leave. People open doors to let someone inside. Some people open the door simply because they want some fresh air, a change of scenery, or to get a better look. Life taught me that every door isn't the same.

There are Kingdom Doors, high doors that Versace had with his emblem, open doors, closed doors, and simple doors. Doors that lead to paths of purpose and those that say do not enter, closed off with caution tape because someone might go back to a place they aren't meant to be. There are doors that have love on the other side and doors that teach you how to love, doors that no man can close and only God can open. There are doors that can only be opened with a key that belongs to you- even doors so small that only a pet can go through. There are windows on doors so you can see before you open it to warn you of the predator of doubt.

Peter was in jail, and as his friends were praying for his release, Roda said Peter was at the door. They didn't believe it, but Roda wasn't wrong. What they were praying for was at the door already knocking. Are you refusing to open the door for purpose because you don't believe it? That knock keeps getting louder because it's a special delivery for you.

Someone Has to Pay   Rolita James

That package sitting on the porch for you can be stolen if you don't open the door if you don't hear the knock. Just because the gift was delivered doesn't mean you got it. Hard knocks taught me that it only takes one knock of procrastination, fear, or doubt to make you miss the meeting of a lifetime.

Life's education is often thought of as hard education. The kind of learning that reinforces survival but let me tell you, I learned some positive things at the University of Hard Knocks, too, like when it's your time to knock, you better knock it out of the park.

Knockdowns, the knock-up, the knock over, but you don't stay down. Just bounce back up like a weeble wobble. By the way, in case you're wondering, what's the story behind this chapter.

Do you remember all of the knock, knock jokes? Too many to keep up with, right? Some were so dry and corny, some were worth nothing more than a chuckle, and maybe one percent were knee slappers. Why did we give knock-knock jokes so much credit and play space in our lives? My grandson said, "Knock-knock," and I said, "Oh no," because I had an idea it might not be funny. Are you cracking up at your own jokes that aren't even funny? The moral of my knock, knock is there was not one joke at my university. I often ignored the knock of peace and golden links, looking for the punch line before the process that led to my maturity, purpose, or even my final destination in that season. The knock of knowing the difference between somebody who wants you or something that has you occupying space vs. somebody who stays in the way so no one else can have you or you don't move on.

Knock . . . . knock

I heard a knock at the door. It was my daughter. When I saw her, my heart knocked with joy. Let that simmer, some knocks are to be continued.

Chapter 9

The touch

"Even 99 cent artificial flowers fade"

For me, it's always been about being on the right track, proof that I'm going in the right direction. It makes me think about the woman with the issue of blood. She told herself that if she could just touch the hem of His garment, she would be made whole. So that's just what she did. She made her way through the crowd for the touch she needed, and that's when Jesus questioned who touched Him. The people with Him assumed it wasn't an intentional touch in such a massive crowd of people, but He knew it was because something happens in touch. In touch, there is an exchange, and neither parties leave the same. There's evidence in touch, and the evidence is the effect that something took place.

There are many different touches. You can be touched by words, by something you saw, or by something you heard. You can be touched by an experience, like an event that has shaped you or someone for the better or worse.

What happens when your hand touches the plow? When you do the work, and you've done all the things you are supposed to, when you're waiting for the manifestation while the sun touches the seed you've put in the ground, and the evidence is the fruit of your labor. It's something you can eat, something that nourishes your body. It brings me back to the peach tree Queenie planted in the middle of the hood. She touched the ground, and the evidence of her right direction touched the hands of those who ate from it. It's the evidence that makes the touch so important.

There's the touch of "do" season and the touch in due season. Meaning if you do the work, in due time, you will produce a harvest. There's the touch of sowing and the touch of reaping. Whatever they touch is, good or bad, there is a price. It costs something. Whether you buy real flowers or the 99 cents bunch, they still both fade eventually, and they both cost whoever bought it something. That's why touch is so important. Authentic touch changes forever. It creates an impact so meaningful that its evidence lives as proof far after the encounter. WOW!

Queenie's touch on my life was evident; it is evident. Her touch on the lives of those she interacted with left prints. I saw the touch of strength in her hands. I heard the touch of protection in her voice. I felt the touch of God in her presence.

You can't tell me someone loves you and doesn't want to touch you or be in your presence. You don't want to be touched by me emotionally, physically, or spiritually? Do you want to be touched by my presents or by my presence? Or are you touched by the image of me just to open it like we do some gifts, use once and never use them again?

See, touch speaks even in silence. You don't have to say a word from your lips. You've never heard a tree grow, have you?

I want you to imagine this; are you with me? I finally resolved in my mind and heart that I would be a single parent, happy it would be just me and my son, Judah. I would do the best I could since being a mom didn't come with an instruction manual. I was already fired from the center once Cortez's mother found out I was pregnant. To think; I was carrying her grandchild. I couldn't understand why she didn't want to see us in a better position. Mind you, I never even called out of work, nor was I ever late. I had always been in great character standing. Honest, loyal, compassionate, and willing to learn more. Now, you tell me who on earth wants the liability of hiring a teenage pregnant girl from the ghetto just to give her medical insurance, a better life for her, her son, and a way out? Upgrade. So public assistance was the way to go. You know what public assistance is, right? Welfare, my friend, insurance, a $400 check a month, and food stamps. The state says they are here to help. Nope, they're here to cripple or paralyze you. I actually wanted to work. I asked for insurance only, but I had to take the entire package if I wanted any public assistance. You aren't allowed just to get the help you need. If you worked, they deducted your minimum wage pay from what you received. You couldn't have a car or a savings account to try to save five dollars or so a month to get out of the rut. If you had any increase, your rent went up. No kidding! People are paying $1,900 in the hood all because they cannot save to get out without trying to beat the system. A system set up to keep its partakers stagnated. Pause and stop before you judge or make a strong decision without 100% of the facts. Please reconsider. Everyone receiving public assistance is not lazy or looking for a handout. Most of us were trying to buy things to help us feel normal, pretty, and like we were worth some value.

Cortez touched me, "You are the only person who I can be me with," and he was the person who spoke to my strength and reminded me of how successful I am supposed to be, he turned out to be the same person that set me up to fail. Those touches are starting to make my skin crawl. Fast forward: Have you ever been in a place of existing where moving forward just meant surviving?

That's how I felt. A girl gotta do what a girl gotta do! Oblivious to the shift that is about to happen in my life for the better; I'm in the bank standing in line wearing the maternity dress that I purchased from the thrift shop because now I'm 7 1/2 months pregnant, and I'm showing. There's no more hiding from the nosey people who really don't care for you, nor about you yet have the nerve to put high expectations on you. My belly, the size of the watermelon, was a whole vibe. In line doing everything I could to keep my head up and act okay, knowing good and well, everything that glitters ain't gold.

Something is on the floor right near my foot. Should I step on it and drag it? Should I pick it up and ask if it belongs to anyone? All I see are numbers. What should I do? While I'm in the valley of indecision, dreaming that this is my lottery ticket out of welfare because this was never the plan in the first place, I'm thinking about the five hundred dollar abortion that Cortez's mother wanted me to have, knowing she fired me and I didn't have any money. Cortez gave me $75 toward an abortion, remembering that he called me and assumed that I went to the abortion clinic alone, checking to see if I took care of that. I said, "I sure did." $75 worth ignorant a$$, replaying it in my head scene by scene only to be startled by a touch on my shoulder. I heard a very distinguished voice say, "Excuse me, your foot is on my . . ." and as my stomach and I turned around. I was now face to face with a man that loved me unconditionally. He said "I'd recognize you anywhere; it's been so long, how are you? Where have you been hiding?" He stepped back and looked me up and down, and said, "Well, well, what do we have here?" Now I'm in between shy and ashamed. It was my Godfather. He said, "By the way, excuse me, your foot is on my driver's license."

Wait. One. Minute.

How many of you thought it was money or a quick pick? Ughhh, My Godfather hugged me, wiped the tears that begin to roll down my face and said, "Let's go to lunch," while wiping his wet hand on his faded shirt. Once again, he said, "Xena, I love you." A touch that I longed for and needed. Sitting inside the restaurant near the fireplace on a cold day with my Godfather, I realized the man is a gentleman, honest, brave, compassionate, and a leader, courageous, unselfish, and loyal, one of great character all of this exuding from his eyes and heart-piercing my inner identity was giving me hope. He reached for my hand, held it in his hand, and said, "Daughter come home. You can live next door, pay less rent and build." He didn't ask any questions.

Goodness, just when I thought I had no more tears, we found my face wet, yet again. "Move in today; we will work everything else out." This was Saturday. I started my new temp job Monday. What??? I woke on Monday to a snowstorm. I remember not having a car or any money for a cab or bus pass, so I had to walk the 5 miles. When I got to the job there was a woman from the Islands; her name was Miss Inez, she introduced herself and asked "Oh baby," in her strong Island accent "may I hug you?" She hugged me and said, "Everything is going to be alright." She touched my belly and said, "Hi, I can't wait to meet you and tell you how special your mom is." She looked at me and said, "Don't worry, baby, I feel God has something for you."

There goes a different kind of touch. I started to feel like I was shifting from surviving to beginning to live. That was a touch of life. We all have a story, and I'm sharing mine in a few books. Please do your best to get them as they unfold. It just crossed my mind: What's your story?

Chapter 10

Fantasy and the fate

"People gonna talk, just make sure it's a lie."

I wondered to myself why I didn't dream anymore. The Lord revealed to me that I no longer dreamed because of the rejection and failure I experienced. Rejection and no's can cause you to stop dreaming- and you think whatever is happening in your life and your reality at a particular time is your conclusion, but what if it's not?

There have been times in my life when my fantasy clashed with fate. What I wanted for me in the way I wanted it to be wasn't in line with my destiny, yet I still sought that thing. If you want something bad enough, you just might get it, and I did, but it didn't fulfill me. What you desire, you pursue. I'm not even including the versions of me that settled where I didn't fight anymore because I was tired of perceived loss. Just because you don't want to fight anymore doesn't mean you don't have an enemy. You're standing still, but the enemy is still attacking, so then you have a bully that won't stop bothering you. What's been bullying you these days?

How many times have you stayed in a place not meant for you? We have all the red flags and see all the signs, but we ignore it or rationalize it because we have convinced ourselves it's different?

Your presence means you cosign. If you are there and you don't agree, you do agree.

My fantasy was I'm not perfect, and my fate concurred. Fantasy being the activity of imagining things, especially those that are impossible or unexpected, and fate being the development of events beyond a person's control destined to happen.

From the first chapter through chapter 9, my intentions are for you to notice that my life did not go as I dreamed or imagined. That fantasy to marry a man tall, dark and handsome, educated, wealthy? I would sacrifice to help him build his dream, have children, and put them in private school, while he'd be involved in the community and travel the world. Whew! The fate. How many of you remember the game scrabble? My life letters were all over the place. From the time I was conceived, my life has been all over the place. I want to start from when I thought I was in control. I quit school in the 12th grade to write black history plays in New York for money; I started modeling for magazines. I got involved with the Hip-Hop scene in the Bronx Underground (playing with fire), hanging with Reggie, pregnant at 19 with my fantasy man only to be abandoned, living on my own with section 8 and welfare working temporary jobs to support my prince. Then married early and had more children, adopted children, had homeless people move in, started an organization, helped my husband at the time to start a business, lived and tried to recreate my fantasy by raising my children and marrying a smart, educated military man that wasn't from my neck of the woods, having family night and cooking three meals a day. But, back to my fate, because I still felt alone. I was still smiling in front of people trying to meet someone else's needs. I met a brother who murdered someone with whom he was serving time. When he was released from prison, I invited him to live with us. Wait, what? Why did you almost judge me? You never did anything where you needed another chance? I know I did. Never judge people by their past. People learn. People change. People move on. A clean canvas? I'll wait. When's the last time you examined yourself? Oh, back to fate. As I was saying, things were spiraling out of control.

I thought I married my best friend, but that was the dream; that was my fantasy. The reality was it would be 30 years before he said good things about me or to me. In my fantasy, the fact was he never said anything nice or did much of anything nice, but I was still so in love.

One time, he looked at me and said, "Wow, you really love me." I couldn't say the same, and I still don't know if he ever really did, but I do know he didn't know my love language. I once thought, how can you give something so much passion and walk away empty? But because of the fantasy, I stayed in it, hoping that my fantasy was my fate.

We are now cheating on one another, not considering what we were building. Our daughter was in question. Women said they were pregnant by him. People were checking for STDs. Did I mention I had an abortion? This fate journey was since I took control of my life, thinking that I would do a better job than Queenie.

I made assumptions because I wanted my dream to be a reality, and I paid the price the entire time. This wasn't the first time I played out my fantasy, but it was the time I learned that you can love someone and still leave. Sometimes you have to go through certain things to get where you need to be.

That was a lot but let me get back to the fate side of things. I am a successful entrepreneur. I've been to

Africa, I spoke to 32 members of Parliament, I became a Mediation Specialist for family services in another country, and I travel the world on missions trips. Are you walking in my shoes during my story, or do you have on your own expensive shoes? The ones made by the one, the only, world traveler, can't escape them, siblings for life; you guessed it, fantasy and fate. I know we all want them to be comfortable when worn. Please don't give up when fantasy and fate have a head-on collision. You are worth the investment for your purpose. Jeremiah 29:11 says, "for I know my plans for you, declares the Lord, plans to prosper you and not to harm you, plans to give you hope and a future." Don't be stuck because of the story you tell yourself. Did you know there's another truth beyond what you've experienced? I've had some great news as my journey matures and continues to unfold daily. Some fantastic things have happened. I wrote this book for you to read and get all in your feelings. I want you to think about your own life, forgive, love, and make a sound decision to live in peace, joy, self-control, and don't take what has happened in your life personally. I realized I've been intoxicated from the womb, intoxicated growing up, intoxicated as a young adult, intoxicated during my marriage, intoxicated as a believer in Christ, intoxicated with infidelity, intoxicated at times raising my children, intoxicated because my siblings died, and intoxicated at my new high paying job. I was intoxicated too while messing with a fine Italian man on his boat traveling the world, dazzling while going to events, hearing him say, "My mother wouldn't understand that I am in love with you because you're black."

I stumbled into an AA meeting one evening. I was introduced to a counselor that laid my life on the table; the truth beyond the truth that I mentioned prior. He introduced me to an amazing sponsor that helped me change and held me accountable. I wanted to live better. I wanted to be different. I feel like you're reading and wondering which AA meeting did I attend. I went to this one with my best friend- AA Always. Available. The counselor was Jesus Christ, and my sponsor was The Holy Spirit. Now you may not start at a meeting; keep searching for the truth beyond your reality. Make sure that you know the differences between fantasy, fate, the truth that you told yourself to believe, and the truth beyond fantasy and fate.

Chapter 11

On my own

"You can't go back and change the beginning but you can start where you are and change the ending."

It had been three years since Queenie passed, but in a moment, memories of her would come rushing in. Although I'm reminded of her often, there was something special about finding a piece of her. As I was organizing some old boxes, I happened to find her old eyeglass case, and I opened it; inside were folded notepapers with handwritten scriptures. With tears welling up in my eyes, I looked up the scriptures she referenced and read them aloud. At that moment alone, I felt so close to Queenie, almost like the scriptures were a message from her to me. I thought about all that I learned from Queenie, all the things she taught me. Queenie had a vision. She was a visionary who took on so much just to give us a good life. She gave me hope, and She taught me that you have to have a vision to see. It seemed like Queenie was always there, which is why I suppose this moment was so special to me. In her absence, she was still teaching; her impact still felt even in this moment alone.

And here I am on my own. How many trials, and victories did you experience on your own? There were times I was on my own throughout my life, even when it didn't feel like it, and times when people were around, but I still felt all alone.
I remember. Queenie made it to my wedding, but Flawless wasn't there. She died alone, giving herself an abortion.

KO wasn't there either.

His wife was upset about dress colors, so she wouldn't let my father walk me down the aisle. I suppose looking back, it could have been resentment for what I represented. I was a reminder of the times he left her all alone. KO felt terrible and was going behind his wife's back, paying my rent, trying to play his part in my life. I let him know it was okay not to come to the wedding. Deep down, I know it hurt him. The truth is it hurts me too, but we both decided to deal with that hurt alone. I will never know how it feels to have my dad walk me down the aisle; that's a walk I took on my own.

There were a lot of big moments when there was no one there with me. When I bought my house, I did that alone.
Even Cortez wasn't with me, y'all remember. I had our baby on my own, while Sister Gingiddy held my hand when it was time to push. People moved in with me, and I was making mistakes and failing, and leaning on my own understanding. I learned when you get called by God, you can't live your salvation in the eyes of someone else. He is going to judge you on your own. You have to work out your own salvation.

No one can do anything by themselves, and yet sometimes we are by ourselves.
Someone died of AIDS on their own.
Someone is celebrating their successes on their own.
My sister was strung out on drugs on her own.
Queenie dealt with the trauma of losing her daughter on her own.

Someone Has to Pay   Rolita James

Queenie raised my siblings and I on her own.

You have to stand on your own sometimes. Lies can be easier to digest than when you have to stand by the truth. We believed we were going to be millionaires one day because we were told Flawless died from malpractice. When my siblings died, I dealt with that truth on my own.

Queenie had still refused to accept the truth. She had to deal with that pain on her own.
That wasn't the only loss Queenie had to deal with on her own.

Do you remember when I told you Queenie had a daughter who was kidnapped, and years later, she found Queenie and wanted to be reunited, but Queenie was dealing with raising us on her own? Well, years after that, Queenie went to visit her daughter for Christmas. At her house. And when I say house, I mean a 14 bedroom house that was more like a mansion. One can only imagine what it felt like to be there after living in housing for so long. Queenie was excited about spending the holiday with her daughter, and when it was time to open gifts and Queenie opened hers, Queenie had to deal with what she unwrapped on her own. Her daughter had gotten her a drawer liner. Yeah, the kind that had one sticky side that you cut to fit the inside of the junk drawer. That kind. Yet Queenie acted like it was a brand new car. A challenging situation, yet even though they were both present in that moment, they dealt with those emotions on their own. Queenie decided to do what she thought best on her own, and this gift that was a sign of unforgiveness was something her daughter decided on her own.

I have a question for you. What are you doing on your own? There are a lot of things when people are on their own. One thing is for sure. You can make it on your own. Think positive. Think big. Stay humble and continuously learn. There's another truth to the truth. I'm talking to the person with the white picket fence, the CEO. I'm talking to the pilot, and the drug dealers too. I'm talking to the addict who started using because their mother abused them, the preacher, and the Presidents of nations, the ones riding slow with the music loud, FBI agents, the man who owns the bodega, and the ones who go in the corner store to play numbers three times a day. I'm also talking to the CIA personnel whose father walked away and the person sitting behind prison walls. I'm talking to the person who just decided to get their life back on track, the one who just took the new job, the one who just got fired, and the person who is thinking of taking the leap of faith and opening their business. I'm talking to the one playing in a game today, but there's no one cheering you on in the bleachers. The game doesn't end, and the scoreboard doesn't stop just because you're on your own.

When you're in the mirror, you are on your own. That's Reflection. As high as you may think of me, you are me. No one escapes being on their own at some point in life. When you escape the crowd and lay down, you are alone, even if you are sleeping next to someone. So many mistakes were made on my own. I learned so many things on my own. There's stuff I did that I didn't want to do on my own while asking myself. How did I get here?

I remember being about 14 years old and taking a train ride down to an amusement park with eight of my friends. We just knew we would have a good time, and we did; rides, swimming, fun, and laughter. We got back on the train, and as the conductor was collecting everyone's ticket, I realized mine wasn't where I had initially put it.

Someone Has to Pay   Rolita James

Now I was getting a little nervous because I already knew none of us had any extra money to buy a new one, and after a few minutes of fumbling with nothing to produce to the conductor, he put me off the train at the next stop, alone. And there I was on my own, in a strange place because none of my friends got off with me. Not one of the eight, and now looking back on that moment in time, I realize there are some journeys you may have started out with people that you will finish alone. There may be a fork in the road you are traveling on, and they will go one way, and you go another. So here I am, just me late at night in a place that's random to me with no money and nobody when this white woman coming out of a bar approaches me. It was the last call for drinks and she asked me if everything was okay. She began a conversation with me, and as I started explaining my situation, she was thinking of a plan. I should mention here because I need to be clear that I am, a black girl from the hood, talking to this wealthy white woman in an affluent neighborhood in the '80s. This isn't a typical scene, but how many people know that when God has a plan, it's not about how it looks? You may be facing things on your own right now, and other people can see it, and to them, it doesn't look good. It might not look good to you either, but it doesn't mean God isn't working.

The woman put 10 pennies in my hand and told me to go into the bar to exchange them for a dime. Take the dime and go to the payphone right on the corner and call the police. The police of each city would then take me to each city line until I got home. That's what Queenie would call a ram in a bush.

Let me pause for a second here and tell you about when I would be a ram in the bush for somebody else years later. One Saturday morning, I met a Jewish man whose car had broken down. Since it was the Sabbath, he couldn't talk to me, call anyone or help himself without breaking his observance of it. I managed to communicate with him and pay for someone to help him without breaking his commitment. It felt good to pay it forward even years later, the help someone extended to me. How are you paying it forward? Now back to the story. So I did just that. And I eventually made it home on my own, a little hurt but a little wiser. I learned a valuable lesson that day about people, friendship, and loyalty. I learned about perspective and how to see a situation for what it is and what it isn't. I paid the price for that wisdom that day, and that white lady paid too. See, I don't know why she was in the bar that late at night on her own. I suppose maybe I didn't think about that until now, and even though she paid it forward by paying my way home that night, who knows what else she was paying for. Some of us might still be paying for the mistakes we made, and some are reaping a whopping harvest of joy for all the tears we sowed in a different season.

We all have stuff. No one is exempt from hard situations. I believe what matters more is how you show up through those challenges. Nothing is free. Even the "free" things are going to cost you something. The issue is that many people think money but time, love, obedience, attention, and loyalty are forms of currency. There's something you should know about this journey. Two things specifically:

You don't have to be scared to walk alone and somebody has to pay. Jesus paid.

Can I ask y'all a question? So who pays?

Made in the USA
Middletown, DE
25 July 2022